JANE AUSTEN

Children's Stories

Dados Internacionais de Catalogação na Publicação (CIP) de acordo com ISBD

A933s Austen, Jane
Sense and sensibility / Jane Austen. – Jandira : W. Books, 2025.
96 p. ; 12,8cm x 19,8cm. – (Jane Austen Children's Stories)

ISBN: 978-65-5294-185-5

1. Literatura infantojuvenil. 2. Romance. 3. Literatura estrangeira. 4. Literatura inglesa. 5. Amor. 6. Preconceito. 7. Inglaterra. I. Título. II. Série.

2025-591 CDD 028.5
CDU 82-93

Elaborado por Vagner Rodolfo da Silva - CRB-8/9410
Índice para catálogo sistemático:
1. Literatura infantojuvenil 028.5
2. Literatura infantojuvenil 82-93

1st edition in 2025
www.cirandacultural.com.br

JANE AUSTEN

Sense and Sensibility

W. Books

Chapter 1

The Dashwood family had lived at Norland for many years. It was a large house in Sussex and the three sisters who lived there loved it very much.

Elinor was the eldest. She was sensible, kind and responsible.

Marianne was the second eldest. Although she was only a couple of years younger than Elinor, their personalities were very different. Marianne was a poetic dreamer.

Lastly, there was Margaret. Margaret had just turned thirteen. She loved her tree house and hiding in the library to listen to grown-up conversations.

Their happy life at Norland ended when their father died. Norland now belonged the girls' half-brother, John. This meant that Elinor, Marianne, Margaret and their mother would have to find somewhere new to live.

Fanny, John's wife, spared no time moving into her new home. She was willing to let her husband's sisters and mother-in-law live at Norland until they found somewhere else. However, she did not like her husband's other plans for the girls.

'My dear, I feel I should give my sisters some money to help them in their new life,' said John one morning. 'My father did ask me to help them after he was gone.'

‘Ha!’ said Fanny, enjoying breakfast at her vast new dining table. ‘Help does not mean *money*. I imagine he was talking about inviting them to stay now and then.’

John Dashwood nodded. He was easily persuaded by his wife and happy to agree with her. ‘I’m sure you are right, my dear,’ he said. ‘Would you mind passing the butter?’

Mrs Dashwood could not understand her stepson’s reluctance to share any of her husband’s wealth but she kept her feelings hidden. Marianne, on the other hand …

'How can anyone be so unfeeling!' she raged, as the sisters and their mother sat in Elinor's bedroom. 'Fanny sees Norland as quite her own now.'

'That's because it is her own, dearest,' said Elinor, calmly.

Elinor had made a list of cottages they could afford to rent. They were far smaller than Norland. So far none of them had met the expectations of her mother and sisters.

'That one is north-facing,' said Mrs Dashwood.

'That one doesn't have a garden!' said Margaret.

'That one only has three bedrooms!' said Marianne.

It seemed that nothing Elinor could do or say would lift her mother and sisters' spirits. Their hearts were broken – but so was hers. As always, however, Elinor's feelings would have to wait. She had to take care of her family first.

Chapter 2

A few weeks after Fanny and John had moved into Norland, Fanny's brother Edward came to stay. Marianne was dreading meeting any relation of Fanny's. However, from the moment he arrived it was clear that Edward was nothing like his sister. Edward was thoughtful and enjoyed reading, but what Marianne liked best about him was how much he seemed to admire Elinor.

During Edward's stay, Elinor took many walks with him. She learnt that he disliked his family's obsession with money. What Edward wished for more than anything was a quiet, country life. Perhaps as a clergyman.

Late one night, Marianne knocked on Elinor's bedroom door. 'Oh good, you're awake,' said Marianne, jumping onto the bed next to Elinor. 'I wanted to talk to you about Edward.'

'Edward?' replied Elinor, innocently.

'Yes! It's true he is terrible at reading poetry aloud, but I can overlook that if you tell me he is to be my brother.'

Elinor lowered the book she was trying to read and stared at her sister. 'Marianne! We are not engaged!' she said. On seeing Marianne's surprise, Elinor continued, 'I admit that I like him. I think highly of him.'

'*Like* him? *Think highly* of him?' Marianne spluttered. 'When *I* fall in love with someone it will not suit such dull words. I believe in love at first sight!'

Elinor laughed. 'Perhaps you will see your love tonight,' she said, playfully throwing a pillow at her sister. 'Sweet dreams!'

As Marianne shut the door to her room, Elinor tried to focus on her book again. It was no good. It may not be passionate enough for Marianne, but Elinor *had* fallen in love with Edward. She believed he felt the same way about her.

Unfortunately, it wasn't only Marianne who had noticed the affection between Elinor and Edward. Fanny had watched them together and she was not pleased. She took the opportunity of talking to Mrs Dashwood when the two of them were having tea.

'My mother has high hopes for my

brothers,' Fanny began, clinking her teaspoon loudly on the side of her cup.

'Is that so?' replied Mrs Dashwood.

'Yes, she expects them to marry very well,' Fanny said. 'Of course she worries that our family's fortune

might attract …' Fanny paused. 'Well, it might appeal to girls who don't have any money of their own …'

Mrs Dashwood flushed. She knew that Fanny was talking about Elinor and Edward. 'Does Mrs Ferrars not wish her sons to marry for love?' she said, trying to control her anger.

Fanny smiled a knowing smile. '*Of course*,' she said. 'She simply expects that they will love girls worthy of them. If you understand me.'

Mrs Dashwood carefully placed her teacup on the table. 'Yes, I understand you.'

Chapter 3

'Who is Sir John Middleton?' Margaret exclaimed. She was lying on the library floor eating an apple while her mother and sisters discussed Mrs Dashwood's news.

Mrs Dashwood had a cousin with a large estate in Devon. On that estate was a cottage that would suit the four

of them perfectly. Mrs Dashwood had received the letter weeks ago, but was only now ready to act on it. She would not stay at Norland and have her daughters insulted by Fanny.

Edward and Elinor managed a quick goodbye before Fanny whisked him away. Marianne cried in each room and tried to argue the importance of taking her piano with them. Elinor reminded her that it would not fit in their new sitting room.

Margaret said goodbye to her tree house and started to make plans for a new one as she climbed into the carriage after her sisters.

As it turned out, Barton Cottage was not as bleak as Marianne had imagined it to be. It was small enough to fit inside the gatehouse at Norland, but it was cosy and had a beautiful view across the valleys and hills.

The Dashwoods had not been in their new house long before they received their first visitor. 'Hello

there!' cried a cheerful voice. Sir John Middleton was walking up the path to Barton Cottage, surrounded by dogs.

Mrs Dashwood and the three girls tumbled out of the house to meet him. 'It was so kind of you to give us the cottage,' began Mrs Dashwood.

'Not at all!' cried Sir John. 'We love company and who better than four new beautiful faces!'

Margaret giggled. Sir John was the liveliest person she had seen in a long time.

He continued, 'I have come to invite you to Barton Park for dinner tomorrow night, once you are settled. I shan't take no for an answer!'

Barton Park was a lovely, red-brick home. It was not as grand as Norland, but it was still very large. At dinner that night was Sir John, his wife Lady Middleton, his mother-in-law Mrs Jennings, and his good friend Colonel Brandon who lived nearby.

After dinner, Marianne delighted everyone by singing and playing the piano.

'Mark my words,' whispered Mrs Jennings to Mrs Dashwood. 'I'll have Colonel Brandon married to one of your daughters before the year is out!'

Mrs Dashwood was shocked. No one in Norland spoke as bluntly as Mrs Jennings.

'I thought he would be a good match for Elinor,' Mrs Jennings continued, ‘as they are closer in age. But he seems quite taken with Marianne.’

Mrs Dashwood looked from Marianne to Colonel Brandon and noticed how closely he was watching her play. Perhaps Mrs Jennings was right …

Chapter 4

A week passed at Barton Cottage. Elinor sewed curtains and Marianne painted a mural around the fireplace. Margaret made excellent progress on her tree house and Mrs Dashwood became quite good at baking bread. Many things had changed for the Dashwoods, but nowhere near enough for Marianne to consider marrying an "old man".

'Colonel Brandon is no more than thirty-five!' laughed Elinor.

'Then you marry him,' Marianne said, moodily.

'She can't! She's in love with Edward,' said Margaret plainly. Elinor stopped laughing. She had not heard from Edward since they had left Norland. Being apart from him was harder than she'd imagined.

‘Come on, you,’ said Marianne, dragging her little sister by the arm. ‘It’s time for a walk!’

Barton Cottage might be small, but the hills around it were vast. Marianne loved exploring them.

'I think we should go back,' said Margaret, after they had been walking for a while. The sky was black and had begun to drizzle.

'No!' cried Marianne. 'By the time we've run down this hill, it's sure to stop.'

Margaret was about to argue when Marianne tripped and rolled to the bottom of the hill. Her dress was soaked and muddy. Her ankle was twisted and she could not stand.

Margaret began to cry. 'Oh, Marianne, what shall I do?'

'Run back to the cottage and–' Before Marianne could say any more, a shadow fell across them.

Elinor stared out of the cottage window for any sign of her sisters. They had been gone far longer than usual and the weather was getting worse. Just then a tall figure appeared. A man. A very soggy Margaret was running after him and in his arms was – Marianne!

While blankets were found for the shivering Marianne, her rescuer explained that he had been out riding when he saw the lady fall. His name was Willoughby and he asked to call again tomorrow to check on Marianne's health.

After Willoughby had left, Marianne sat in a chair by the fire resting her leg. Her mind, however, was racing.

'It was so romantic, Elinor!' she cried. 'I owe him my life!'

Elinor smiled. 'I don't think people often die of a twisted ankle, dearest,' she replied. Marianne wasn't listening. Her mind was full of Willoughby.

From the morning after her fall, Marianne and Willoughby were inseparable. He brought her flowers and a book of poetry to read. When she was strong enough, he took her riding. Willoughby was even invited to dinner at Barton Park where everyone liked him. Everyone except Colonel Brandon.

Chapter 5

It was a beautiful summer's day and Colonel Brandon invited everyone for a picnic on his estate at Delaford. Sir John, Lady Middleton and Mrs Jennings went there in their carriage followed by the Dashwoods. Marianne and Willoughby had raced ahead on their own.

At Delaford Colonel Brandon was just about to lead the party to the picnic spot when the sound of urgent galloping approached. Every head

turned to see a messenger jump off his horse. He handed a letter to Colonel Brandon.

'I must go to London!' Colonel Brandon announced as soon as he had read the letter. 'This very moment.'

'Oh Colonel, surely it can wait until after the picnic!' said Mrs Jennings.

'It cannot,' said Colonel Brandon. 'I have not a moment to lose. Forgive me.'

The party could only watch as Colonel Brandon galloped away on his horse. Then, for a moment, there was silence.

'Never mind!' said Sir John, clapping his hands together cheerfully. 'Let us picnic at Barton Park, instead!'

Sir John did not question his friend leaving so suddenly, and Elinor thought he seemed keen to distract others from questioning it

either. Perhaps Sir John knew that the answers were too private to come from anyone but Brandon himself.

As the sun began to set behind Barton Cottage, Willoughby helped the Dashwoods to take their picnic things back into the house.

'How I love this cottage,' Willoughby sighed. 'If I could, I would pull down Combe Magna and rebuild it to look just the same!'

Everyone laughed at the thought of Willoughby pulling down his grand house to build a tiny cottage instead.

'Mrs Dashwood,' said Willoughby, suddenly serious. 'May I ask your permission to talk to Miss Marianne alone tomorrow?'

Marianne's heart leapt. Secretly she took hold of Elinor's hand and squeezed it. There was only one reason why a young man would ask to talk to a young lady alone. He was going to ask Marianne to marry him!

'Of course, Willoughby,' replied Mrs Dashwood.

Chapter 6

Mrs Dashwood, Elinor and Margaret left Marianne at home when they went to church. They expected to return after Willoughby's visit and find Marianne running from the house to show off her engagement ring. But everything was quiet.

Elinor could see her sister's outline through the front parlour window, pacing frantically.

'Something is wrong,' said Elinor, worriedly.

Willoughby burst out of the front door. When he saw the three Dashwoods he bowed quickly. 'I'm afraid I must go to London,' he said. His eyes were red. 'I ...' But Willoughby could not explain further. 'Forgive me,' he said, and walked hurriedly down the path.

In the days that followed, Marianne refused to talk about what had happened. Willoughby had gone but he would come back, she insisted. In the meantime Marianne cried and spent a good deal of time staring out of the parlour window.

Mrs Jennings announced that her nieces were coming to stay at Barton Park. Anne and Lucy Steele were about the same age as Elinor and Marianne. Mrs Jennings was sure that they would cheer Marianne up.

Anne Steele loved to talk. She could talk on a hundred different topics in the space of an hour and never ran out of conversation. Lucy smiled and

nodded at her sister's stories, adding to them occasionally. There was one evening, however, when Lucy felt the need to talk without her sister.

'Elinor? May I talk with you privately?' asked Lucy. Elinor was confused, but nodded and led Lucy to a quiet part of the Middleton's drawing room. The rest of the party were busy playing cards.

'Do you know Mrs Ferrars?' asked Lucy in a hushed voice. 'I understand your brother is married to her daughter.'

'Fanny? Yes,' replied Elinor. 'But I don't know her mother at all. Do you?'

'Oh no,' said Lucy. 'We are not acquainted. However there may be a time when we become very closely connected.'

Elinor began to understand. 'Do you mean … Do you mean that you are engaged to Robert Ferrars? Fanny's brother?'

Lucy looked confused. 'No, I have never met him,' she said. 'I speak of *Edward* Ferrars. We have been engaged for four years.'

Elinor could not believe it. Edward. *Her* Edward. Engaged to Lucy Steele!

'Have I upset you?' Lucy asked. 'Perhaps I should not have revealed such a secret when we don't know each other that well.'

Elinor calmed herself and swallowed hard. 'You have not upset me, I assure you,' she lied.

'I knew I could talk to you,' Lucy said, placing a hand over Elinor's. 'Edward told me all about you. I would have been jealous, but I know he loves only me.'

Lucy stared at Elinor. Elinor stared back. She would not let her feelings show. She would not throw Lucy Steele's hand off her own and leave the room.

But, oh, how she wanted to.

Chapter 7

Mrs Dashwood despaired. Her two eldest daughters were now equally unhappy. Marianne was still missing Willoughby, but Mrs Dashwood did not know the reason for Elinor's sadness. Elinor was bound by Lucy's

secrecy. She had to carry on as though nothing had happened.

Mrs Dashwood was relieved when Mrs Jennings suggested that Elinor and Marianne join her for a few weeks in London. There would be balls to attend and plays to watch. All kinds of fun things to occupy the elder Dashwood sisters.

Marianne jumped at the chance because Willoughby was in London. Elinor also agreed. She was happy to think she would be away from Lucy Steele and her sister, until Mrs Jennings revealed that they would be coming too.

Immediately after they arrived at Mrs Jennings's smart London house, Marianne wrote a note to Willoughby. Marianne then insisted on waiting at home each morning to see if he would visit her. She felt certain he would come, and finally a knock was heard.

'He is here!' Marianne gasped, smoothing her dress. 'Oh Elinor, it really is him!'

However, as the door to Mrs Jennings' parlour opened, it was not Willoughby but Colonel Brandon who entered.

'Oh. Colonel,' said Marianne, unable to hide her disappointment. 'Excuse me.' Marianne brushed past the Colonel and hurried upstairs.

'She is a little unwell,' said Elinor. She was trying to excuse Marianne's behaviour. She was not sure Colonel Brandon believed her, but he claimed he was glad to talk to Elinor alone.

'Miss Dashwood, tell me,' Colonel Brandon asked. 'Is your sister engaged to Mr Willoughby?'

Elinor was surprised by the Colonel's question, but she knew why he had to ask it. He was in love with Marianne.

'She has not told me so,' Elinor replied. 'But I am certain of their affection for each other.'

Colonel Brandon nodded slowly. 'Then I hope he deserves her,' he said.

However, his tone suggested that he doubted it.

All Marianne's hopes now rested on seeing Willoughby at a ball they had been invited to attend. Anne and Lucy Steele were excited to see so many people they knew there, while Marianne feared she might never find Willoughby in the crowd. She scanned the people dancing and talking for any sign of him.

Their little group soon found Fanny and John Dashwood.

'How lovely to see you,' said Fanny to her sisters-in-law. Fanny's face did not match her words. 'Who have you brought with you?'

Elinor introduced Lucy and Anne Steele. Lucy could barely contain her excitement at being introduced to Edward's sister. When Elinor noticed that Marianne had disappeared into the crowd, she happily excused herself to go and look for her.

Chapter 8

Elinor found Marianne staring at a group of well-dressed people in the corner of a small room off the dancing hall. 'It is Willoughby!'

Marianne breathed. 'He cannot have seen me! *Willoughby*!' Marianne called out. More than one head turned at her raised voice.

Willoughby excused himself from the group. 'Miss Dashwood, Miss Marianne,' he said, formally. 'I hope your family is well.'

Elinor started to answer but Marianne laughed. 'Goodness

Willoughby, you talk as if we are strangers. What is wrong with you?'

Willoughby looked over the top of Marianne's head. It was as though looking straight at her might melt the coldness from his face. 'Excuse me,' he said, bowing once more. 'I must return to my friends.'

Marianne was in shock. This was not the Willoughby she knew. It was as though he had changed into a different person.

'Elinor?' Marianne said. 'Why won't he come to me? I ...'

The heat of the room and her meeting with Willoughby

overwhelmed Marianne and she began to feel faint.

'May I help?' Colonel Brandon had been watching the dreadful scene unfold. He took Marianne's arm. With Elinor on the other side, they helped Marianne out of the ball and away from Willoughby.

On their return to Mrs Jennings's, Marianne wrote a letter to Willoughby. She would not tell Elinor what it said.

In fact she did not speak at all until the following morning at breakfast, when she received a reply. In the privacy of her room, Marianne read the letter.

Miss Dashwood,
I am sorry if I have caused you any distress. I hold your family in high regard, but I apologise if I have given you the impression that I feel more for you than I do. My affections have long belonged to Miss Grey, who I am to marry very soon.

I have returned the letters you have kindly sent to me.
Mr John Willoughby

Marianne then read the letter aloud to Elinor. 'But my darling, were you not engaged?' Elinor asked when she had finished.

Marianne shook her head miserably. 'I always thought he would ask, but he never did.' A flood of tears followed. Elinor tried her best to comfort her sister. She was not helped by the arrival of Mrs Jennings, who did not seem surprised to find Marianne crying.

'I have just heard the news!' she said. 'Poor dear. Willoughby is to marry Miss Grey who has £50,000 to her name.'

Marianne cried harder.

'There, there, my dear,' said Mrs Jennings. 'He is not the only young man in the world.' Then she bustled out of the bedroom in search of food to cheer Marianne up. Elinor knew that only one thing would help Marianne: to get out of London as soon as possible.

Chapter 9

Elinor was slumped on a chair in Mrs Jennings's parlour. She had spent most of the night holding Marianne while she wept and she had risen early to write a letter to Colonel

Brandon. She expected him to call at Mrs Jennings's house at any moment.

'How is Marianne?' asked Lucy as she entered the parlour. 'I do feel sorry for her. I would be devastated if my Edward treated me so badly.'

Elinor was not in the mood to listen to Lucy's declarations of love for Edward. She was relieved when she heard the front door open as she was certain it would be Colonel Brandon. However it was Edward Ferrars himself who entered.

'Elinor,' he said, smiling warmly. 'Oh, and Lucy!' Edward looked from Elinor to Lucy and for a moment he was lost for words.

'I am glad to see you, Edward,' said Lucy. 'How clever of you to find out I was staying with Mrs Jennings!'

Edward looked confused. 'Ah, well,' he began. 'I actually came to see Miss Dashwood. To invite her and her family to dinner with my brother, Robert.'

Lucy's eyes narrowed and she looked at Elinor.

'Thank you,' replied Elinor in a calm voice, even though her insides were trembling. 'But I am hoping to return home to Barton Cottage soon. This very day if we can.'

Edward looked disappointed.

'I can come,' Lucy said, a little too loudly. 'I should like to meet your brother. In fact, why don't we go now?'

Lucy linked her arm with Edward and walked him out of the room. Edward looked back at Elinor before the door closed behind them.

The next time it opened was for Colonel Brandon. Elinor had asked for his help getting Marianne home in her letter.

'Mrs Jennings is to visit her daughter and her new baby,' Elinor explained to him now. 'The Palmer's estate is called Cleveland, which is

not far from Barton. Mrs Jennings has offered to take us with her.'

'Then I shall take you the rest of the way home,' replied Colonel Brandon.

Elinor felt as though a huge weight had been lifted. Not only would she get Marianne away from London, she would also get herself away from Edward and Lucy.

'Miss Dashwood, I have something to tell you that may make your sister feel a little better,' added Colonel Brandon. 'I believe Mr Willoughby truly cared for Marianne and wanted to marry her.'

Elinor stared at Colonel Brandon. 'How do you know such a thing?' she asked.

Colonel Brandon took a deep breath. 'A long time ago, I was in love with a girl very like your sister,' the Colonel began. 'She was called Eliza. We could not marry and we lost touch, but I never forgot her. When I found her again, she was alone and had a little girl called Beth. Eliza was ill – dying – so I promised to look after Beth for her.

‘I found a loving family for Beth and made sure she had everything she could ever want. But a few months ago, she went missing. Then, on the day of the picnic, I learnt that she had finally been found. Only by that time she was pregnant. Miss Dashwood, I think you can guess who the father is.’

‘Willoughby?’ Elinor gasped.

Colonel Brandon nodded sadly. ‘When his family found out, they stopped his money. So he found himself a rich wife. However, his acquaintances tell me he would have married Marianne if he could.’

Chapter 10

Marianne packed her trunk slowly and carefully. Her eyes were still pink from crying. Elinor had told her everything that Colonel Brandon had said. None of it made Marianne feel any better.

When Elinor and Marianne were finished with their preparations, they wondered where Mrs Jennings had got to. They were due to leave for the Palmers any moment.

'Well!' said Mrs Jennings, blustering through the hallway. 'Sorry I am late. I have just been with our darling Lucy!' Mrs Jennings stopped to catch her breath. 'What do you think? Lucy has been secretly engaged to Edward Ferrars for *years*!'

Marianne's eyes shot to Elinor, but Elinor refused to look back.

'Anne accidentally let it slip to Edward's family and now they are in uproar,' said Mrs Jennings. 'Edward's mother has cut off his money but he is standing by Lucy. Goodness! What a way to end a trip.'

It took Mrs Jennings just under half an hour to fall asleep in the carriage. As soon as Marianne heard her snores, she whispered to Elinor. 'How long have you known about Edward and Lucy?'

'Almost as long as we have known the Steeles,' replied Elinor.

'But you have been so caught up with me and *my* feelings,' said Marianne, 'that you kept it to yourself?'

'I was not allowed to speak of it,' said Elinor, quietly. 'You could not have known.'

'Both our hearts have been broken,' said Marianne, placing her head on her sister's shoulder. 'But we always have each other.'

Elinor and Marianne set out with Mrs Jennings and Colonel Brandon for Cleveland. Once they arrived, they quickly got to know their new hosts. Mrs Palmer was loud and bubbly, just like her mother, Mrs Jennings. Mr Palmer was very serious and only

said a few words at a time. Their new baby was beautiful and a welcome distraction from the drama the sisters had left in London.

'Of course, Mother has told me of your horrid situation,' Mrs Palmer said to Marianne. 'I wish we could plant tall trees to block our view of Mr Willoughby's house!'

Marianne sat up straighter. 'Combe Magna is nearby?' she asked.

‘Yes,’ replied Mrs Palmer. ‘But I have put you in a room facing away from it, so you won’t be reminded of him.’

Elinor sighed. If Mrs Palmer had said nothing at all, Marianne would not have been reminded of him in the first place.

After lunch, Elinor sat staring out at the rain. ‘Where is Marianne?’ asked Colonel Brandon, suddenly.

‘The library, I believe,’ replied Elinor.

‘She is not there, nor in her room,’ said Colonel Brandon. ‘I sent a maid to bring her some tea when she did not come down to lunch.’

'She went for a walk,' said Mr Palmer from behind his newspaper. 'I think we can all guess where she was headed.'

Chapter 11

A search party was organised and Colonel Brandon led the way. The rain grew heavier as Elinor waited. Marianne had been gone for hours.

Elinor made herself sip the tea Mrs Palmer gave her. She tried to smile and nod as Mrs Jennings wittered on about broken hearts. Inside she was sick with worry.

Finally, Elinor could see a figure approaching the house through the window. She blinked at the image, remembering watching a figure emerge through the rain once before. This time it was Colonel Brandon carrying Marianne, as Willoughby had done many months before.

Elinor rushed to the hallway as they entered. 'She has a fever. She needs to get dry and warm, quickly,' Colonel Brandon said, sweeping Marianne up the stairs to her room.

'I shall call a doctor,' said Mr Palmer.

The fire in Marianne's room blazed and she was dressed in a clean, dry nightgown. She drifted in and out of consciousness, her temperature rising.

The doctor Mr Palmer had called was a kind

and knowledgeable man. He stayed by Marianne's bedside almost as long as Elinor. Whenever the bedroom door opened, Colonel Brandon could be seen outside, anxiously waiting for news.

'My dear Elinor, perhaps you should rest?' suggested Mrs Jennings. 'One of us can stay with Marianne for a while.'

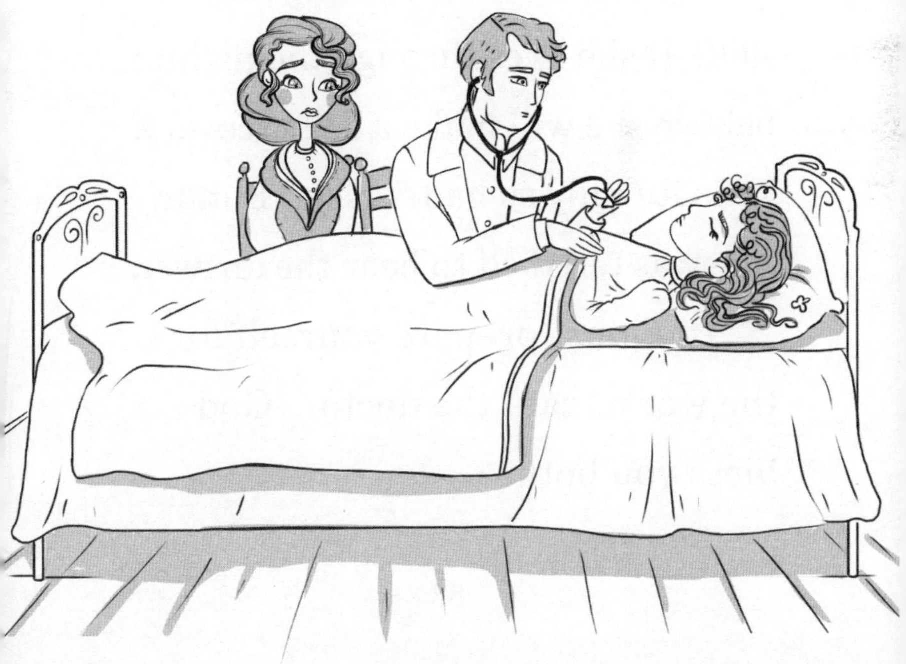

'Thank you,' said Elinor as she gently wiped Marianne's forehead. 'But I would like to stay.'

Finally, the doctor packed up his bag. 'There is nothing more I can do for the young lady,' he said. 'If she lives through the night, I believe she will make a full recovery.'

'Is it really so bad?' asked Elinor. She was terrified to hear the answer.

'You must prepare yourself for the worst,' said the doctor. 'God bless you both.'

Marianne had not woken except to ask for her mother. Fearing the worst, Colonel Brandon took a carriage to fetch her and Margaret. Who knew if they would return in time?

Once she was alone in Marianne's room, Elinor began to shake. She could not lose her sister. She was

her other half. Marianne was happy while Elinor was serious. Marianne was artistic while Elinor was practical. They completed each other more than any man ever could.

Elinor stayed awake all night and held Marianne's hand. In the morning Elinor thought that Marianne's lips and cheeks were rosier. Her breathing seemed steadier. In the afternoon, Marianne opened her eyes. 'Elinor?' she said.

'Yes, I am here!' replied Elinor. By evening the rest of their family was too. Mrs Dashwood and

Margaret cried with relief to find Marianne alive and on the mend.

Later, Marianne asked for Colonel Brandon. She took his hand as he neared.

'Thank you, Colonel Brandon,' Marianne said warmly. 'Thank you.'

Chapter 12

When Marianne was well enough to be moved, the Dashwoods returned to Barton Cottage. Colonel Brandon

visited often and his attentions to Marianne were no longer unwelcome. In time it was the opposite.

Elinor was busy sewing a little pair of curtains for Margaret's tree house when she spotted a horse on the lane. 'Marianne!'she called. 'Colonel Brandon is here!'

'It is not Colonel Brandon,' said Margaret from high in the tree house. 'It's Edward!'

Elinor and Mrs Dashwood looked at each other in surprise. They quickly tidied away the sewing and called everyone into the parlour just as Edward arrived.

'It is lovely to see you, Edward,' said Mrs Dashwood.

'Thank you. I wish I could have come sooner,' he replied. A long silence settled over the group.

'May we congratulate you, Edward,' said Mrs Dashwood. Edward looked confused.

'Mrs Ferrars is not with you?' asked Elinor.

'No, my mother is in London,' replied Edward.

'I meant your wife, Mrs Edward Ferrars,' said Elinor.

'Then you have not heard?' Edward asked. 'I think you mean Mrs *Robert* Ferrars. Lucy married my brother.'

Elinor clasped her hand to her mouth to stop herself from crying out.

Edward continued. 'It seems she and Robert grew attached to each other in London. When she heard that my brother was to inherit my mother's fortune instead of me, she found herself more in love with him than ever.'

Elinor's feelings could not be hidden any longer. She fled into the garden.

Edward followed. 'My dear Elinor, I became engaged when I was very young. I knew nothing of love. I only knew when I met you and by then I had already given my word to Lucy. I was not free to be with you until … until now …'

To Elinor it seemed that every tear she had held in that past year escaped her then. Only now they had been transformed into tears of joy.

Colonel Brandon and Marianne were married. Marianne realised that first loves were not the only kind, and love at first sight was not always the truest. True love was caring without knowing if it would ever be returned. True love was kindness and generosity that extended even to her family.

They were married at the Delaford church by Mr Edward Ferrars. His wife, Elinor, was the bridesmaid. Colonel Brandon had made Edward the clergyman of his estate when Edward's mother left him penniless. There Edward and Elinor were able to live the happy, simple life they had always wanted.

Mrs Dashwood and Margaret continued to live nearby at Barton Cottage. Margaret finished her tree house and declared that if she fell in love, it would be a far less complicated business than her sisters'.